W9-BNZ-714

Peg-a-Leg

Peg-a-Leg

THE COBBLER OF DUNSOON

by LIN CUTLER

Illustrated by Henry Stahlhut

Alfred A. Knopf

New York

Dedicated to
PROFESSOR EARL L. VANCE,
Florida State University, who liked Peg-a-Leg, gave him a pat on the back, and inspired him to go on his adventures.

This is a Borzoi Book
Published by Alfred A. Knopf, Inc.

 Manufactured in the United States of America. Published simultaneously in Canada by the Ryerson Press.

First Edition

PEG-A-LEG, the cobbler, had just finished making a pair of shoes. He placed them side by side on the counter and stepped back to admire them. He looked at them this way and he looked at them that way. No matter which way he looked at them, they looked so wonderful that his chest began to swell and swell and swell until it was almost ready to burst with pride.

Feeling that he had to share his pride with someone, he darted over to the doorway leading to the rest of his house and called out to his wife, "Ho, Dilly! Hey, Dilly! Here, Dilly! Please, Dilly! If you want to see the best cobbler, the greatest cobbler, the cleverest cobbler in all Dunsoon, you had better come into the shop this very instant."

Good wife Dilly was too busy in her kitchen making bread to be bothered, but Peg-a-leg made such a great racket jumping and dancing and skipping about that she came partway into the shop to see what could be the matter.

PEG-A-LEG
COBBLER

"Did I hear someone call himself the cleverest cobbler in all Dunsoon?" she asked. "What nonsense! Since you are the only cobbler in Dunsoon, you might just as readily be called the *worst* cobbler in all Dunsoon."

"But, Dilly, dear wife! Isn't this the grandest pair of shoes you've ever laid eyes on?" Here Peg-a-leg became quiet for a moment and heaved a great, deep, heartbreaking sigh.

"Now what's the trouble?" asked Dilly. "One minute you're as jumpy as a garden bug; the next, you are as sighful as an old bellows."

"Dear me!" sighed Peg-a-leg once more. "To think that I am charging only five dollars for these shoes!"

"That's all they're worth. How much should you charge for a five-dollar-pair of shoes?"

"Only five dollars for the most beautiful, the best-made shoes in all the world! They are worth ten dollars at the very, very least," declared Peg-a-leg with still another sigh.

"Honestly, Peg-a-leg! I've often thought your pride would be the end of you. But now I'm beginning to fear that your greed will be the death of you."

"But, Dilly," Peg-a-leg began to say, when suddenly a great shadow darkened the small shop.

Peg-a-leg turned himself completely around and looked through the small panes of glass of his shop window. He could hardly believe what he saw. Dilly looked out, too, and was so surprised that her mouth flew open and stayed open.

Outside, a great coach drawn by six white chargers came to a grinding halt. While the horses champed and pawed the ground restlessly with their hoofs, a footman beside the driver jumped down smartly and held open the door of the coach. From the dickey seat at the back, a second footman jumped down briskly and held open the door of Peg-a-leg's shop. Very slowly, and with great dignity, a noble personage arose from the deep cushions of the coach and made his way into Peg-a-leg's shop. Once inside, he stopped, resting his gloved hands on the head of his tall walking-stick.

For a long moment he looked about him. Then, looking high over Peg-a-leg's head, he said, "I take it you are Peg-a-leg, the cobbler of Dunsoon."

"Oh, yes, Your Highness! Yes, Your Excellency! I am Peg-a-leg—the best cobbler, the greatest . . ."

"Yes, yes, yes! Of course! I am Lord of the King's Wardrobe. The King requests that you appear before him without delay."

The Lord of the King's Wardrobe turned himself about, moved slowly out of the shop, and stepped into his great coach where he sank half out of sight into the downy cushions. One footman climbed jauntily onto the dickey. The other footman jumped up neatly beside the driver who took his foot off the brake and cracked his whip crisply. The horses leaped forward, and the coach rolled merrily out and away.

Inside the shop, Dilly still stood with her mouth hanging wide open. Not so with Peg-a-leg. He shook himself and ran to the door to gaze after the departing coach, then he began to whistle and dance and skip about.

"Did you hear that, Dilly?" he said. "The King! The King! The *King of Dunsoon* wants to see me! Me, Peg-a-leg, the cobbler of Dunsoon!"

All at once Peg-a-leg sat down on his workstool, dropped his elbows on his knees, and his chin on his cupped hands, and thought and thought. The more he thought, the more puzzled he became. The more he was puzzled, the more worried he got.

"I wonder why the King wants to see me," he said aloud at last. "I've paid my taxes, so it can't be that. There's no war going on, so he can't want me to be a soldier. If the King wants me, it must be because I am a cobbler. Of course! What else could it be?

"Can it be that the King wants his shoes mended? Prue-true! Kings very rarely have their shoes mended. Can it be that there's something wrong with the last pair of shoes I made for him? No! That can't be it. Nothing is ever wrong with shoes that I make. No, never! Then, the only thing left is that the King must want to order a pair of new shoes."

When Peg-a-leg had decided what it was that the King must want of him, his eyes grew bright. He rubbed his hands together with glee, and he danced and skipped about his shop more merrily than before.

"Did you hear that, Dilly?" he shouted. "Did you hear that? The King wants to order a pair of new shoes."

Dilly closed her mouth, but opened it immediately to say, "I heard nothing of the kind, Peg-a-leg. All I heard is that the King wants to see you. And you'd better hurry, if you ask me. The King does not like to be kept waiting. And most of all, he does not like to be disappointed."

Peg-a-leg continued to dance and sing:

"A pair of new shoes!
A pair of new shoes!
The King will choose
A pair of new shoes.
I'm going at noon
To the King of Dunsoon,
To make him, to take him
A pair of new shoes.
I'll peg and I'll stitch.
Who'll beg? I'll be rich!
What glorious news!
What wonderful news!
The King will order
A pair of new shoes!"

"Do you hear me, Dilly?" Peg-a-leg said, beside himself with joy. "We're going to be rich! Now, I wonder how much to charge the King for a pair of new shoes. I am getting five dollars for these I've just made. Can I charge only five dollars for a pair of shoes for a king? No, the King will want special shoes, extra-special shoes—*King's shoes!* I'll be able to charge him ten dollars. No, I'll charge him twenty dollars. No, I'd better charge him ten dollars for each shoe. That won't sound as much as twenty dollars all at once. Yes, that's a good price. Ten dollars for each shoe."

"King or no king," declared Dilly, "a pair of shoes should cost no more than five dollars."

Peg-a-leg may have heard her but he paid no attention.

"Now, let me see," he said. "What will I need? Leather, extra fine and extra fancy, should cost me about two dollars. Pegs, thread, a new needle or two, polish, laces, wax, this and that, and my time and labor and skill, of course, will come to about two or three dollars more. That will leave me, let me see—hm–hm–hm—exactly so. Yes, that will leave me a very nice profit. Very good. Very good! Very, very, *very* good!" Turning to Dilly, Peg-a-leg said, "Do you hear me, Dilly?"

"Yes, I heard you, Peg-a-leg. All I can say is that you are being greedy. No good comes of being that way. I warn you, Peg-a-leg! Don't be greedy!"

"Greedy-heedy, greedy-needy," replied Peg-a-leg airily. "Kings have lots of money. Twenty dollars it is."

Peg-a-leg danced over to the wall and took down a bag. He skipped over to a drawer and got a piece of crayon. He waltzed over to the counter and picked up some sheets of heavy paper. He rolled up the paper and put it in the bag, tossed in the crayon, and pulled the strings tight. Then with the bag over his shoulder and his hat on his head, he waved a hand in good-by to Dilly, and skipped out of the door of his little shop.

He danced up one street and waltzed down the next, humming, whistling, or singing as he went. In this way, waltzing, dancing, or skipping; singing, humming, or whistling; Peg-a-leg soon came to the gates of the royal palace. Here a most wonderful change came over him. He became very serious. It was not every day that Peg-a-leg came to visit the King.

Peg-a-leg walked through the palace gates, along the path, and up the white marble steps to the great front doors of the palace itself. He took the big, brass knocker in both his hands and gave a wee, double knock. After a while, a doorman opened one of the doors, stuck out his head as far as one eye, and looked Peg-a-leg over from head to foot.

Peg-a-leg took off his cap politely, bowed, and said, "I'm Peg-a-leg. Peg-a-leg, the cobbler. The King sent for me."

"Oh, yes! You're Peg-a-leg, the cobbler. The King sent for you. You'll go to the side door." And the doorman shut the door in Peg-a-leg's face.

So Peg-a-leg went to the side door and rapped with his knuckles. A servant opened the door just a crack and stuck out one eye and the tip of his nose. He looked Peg-a-leg over from foot to head.

Peg-a-leg said to him, "I'm Peg-a-leg, the cobbler. The King sent for me."

"Quite right! You're Peg-a-leg, the cobbler. The King sent for you. You'll go to the back door." And the servant shut the side door in his face.

Peg-a-leg went around to the back of the castle, took a healthy kick at the back door, and said, "I'm Peg-a-leg, the cob . . ." – but the door flew open at his kick. As there was no one to meet him or greet him or shut the door in his face, Peg-a-leg walked right in. He made his own way up a narrow flight of winding stairs and came at last to the King's private chamber.

The King was sitting in his great chair with his stocking feet stretched out straight before him. Side by side on the floor between his feet stood his shoes.

"Good-day, Your Majesty!" said Peg-a-leg.

"Come in, Peg-a-leg, come in. Glad to see you," replied the King without getting up.

"Your Majesty sent for me?"

"Yes, Peg-a-leg, I did. Peg-a-leg, what do you think of these shoes?

Peg-a-leg picked up the shoes and looked them over very carefully. "Very good shoes they are, Your Majesty. If you'll excuse me for saying it, Your Majesty, I always make good shoes. Nothing is ever wrong with a shoe *I* make, Your Majesty."

"Yes, yes, they're all right as shoes go," declared the King. "The question is, do I need a new pair?"

Peg-a-leg looked at the shoes again; toes and heels, inside and outside, soles and uppers, and laces and tongues. The King waited patiently. At last, Peg-a-leg said, "Well, no, Your Majesty. And, then again, perhaps, yes, Your Majesty. That is, it depends, Your Majesty. As there is still a great deal of wear in these shoes, I would say, no, Your Majesty. But, as they are a trifle worn, I would say that they are good enough for everyday wear, but for court days, special days, and holidays, Your Majesty, I would say, yes, Your Majesty, you *do* need a pair of new shoes."

"HM-m-m-m," said the King stroking his lip. "How much would a pair of new shoes cost?"

"Let me see," began Peg-a-leg. "Leather—extra fancy, laces, pegs, thread, wax, needles. Three and three make six—and four make ten. Ten times two make twenty, which could include my profit, divided by two—yes, yes! Ten dollars a shoe, Your Majesty."

"What!" exclaimed the King. "Ten dollars a shoe? Why, that makes twenty dollars for the pair. Isn't that a little high, Peg-a-leg?"

"Yes, Your Majesty, it is a trifle high, but this will be an extra-special pair of shoes. I will make a pair of shoes for you, Your Majesty, the like of which I have never made before."

"Well, I don't know. Twenty dollars is a great deal of money even for a king to have to pay for a pair of shoes. I'll have to ask the Lord of the Treasury."

The Lord of the Treasury was sent for. The King said to him, "I have been thinking of ordering a pair of new shoes. They will cost twenty dollars. Can I afford to get a pair of new shoes today?"

"No, Your Majesty. I am afraid not, Your Majesty. The Queen got some new clothes this week."

"Well, I guess that settles it," the King said sadly. "Although, I did want a pair of new shoes. I'll have to keep on using these until they wear out and then get them mended, I suppose."

Hearing this, Peg-a-leg's hands went up into the air with horror. "Oh, no, Your Majesty!" he gasped. "Think of the King of Dunsoon wearing shoes that have been mended!"

"Oh, I don't know," replied the King, "lots of people have their shoes mended. I'm the King. If I wanted to have my shoes mended, I would and that's all there would be to it. Still, I did want to have a pair of new shoes. When can I afford to have a pair of new shoes?" he asked, turning to the Lord of the Treasury.

The Lord of the Treasury took out a small book

from his pocket, opened it, turned a few pages, and said, "Some money is expected to come in the day after tomorrow, Your Majesty."

Peg-a-leg hurried to say, "Oh, Your Majesty, it will take me at least that long to make your shoes, Your Majesty. I have to be especially careful with shoes I make for you, Your Majesty. It would not do to have anything wrong with your shoes, Your Majesty."

"Very well," said the King. "I'll order a pair of new shoes. And, Peg-a-leg, since you are charging me twenty dollars for them, they had better be better than ever."

"Oh, yes, Your Majesty," Peg-a-leg promised. "I will make a pair of shoes for you the like of which has never been seen in all Dunsoon."

Peg-a-leg opened his bag, took out his pattern paper, and spread it flat on the floor. "And now, Your Majesty," he said, "if it pleases you, I would like to take your measure."

The King got up and stood on the paper in his stocking feet. He locked his thumbs in his belt and looked about him proudly, as if to say, "Look at me! I'm the King of Dunsoon! I'm going to get a pair of new shoes!"

Peg-a-leg took the crayon and traced around the King's feet very carefully. When he had done this, he rolled up the pattern, packed his bag, and took his leave of the King. He hurried back to his shop and set to work. He took a pair of shears and cut out the paper pattern. Then he put the pattern on a piece of leather and traced around it. This time he took his sharpest cobbler's knife and cut and cut away until he had the soles for the two shoes. Now he fell to work and shaped the uppers of the finest, softest leather he had and fitted them to the soles. Without losing a single minute he cut, stitched, sewed, hammered, and pegged away steadily all that day, all that night, and all the next day until he had the shoes all finished.

"There!" said Peg-a-leg, wiping the sweat away from his forehead. He took the shoes in his hands and looked them over this way and that. "They are most certainly the best shoes I ever made. One is as good as the other," he said to himself proudly. He went to sleep and slept soundly, dreaming that he made ever more wonderful, more beautiful shoes. He gloated as he charged thirty, forty, fifty, and even one hundred dollars a pair for them. The next day Peg-a-leg awoke, dressed himself in his best clothes, put the King's shoes into a black velvet bag, and hurried off to the palace.

He knocked on the front door and said, "I'm Peg-a-leg, Cobbler to the King! I'm bringing the King's new shoes."

"Oh, yes!" the doorman answered. "You're Peg-a-leg, the cobbler, bringing the King a pair of new shoes. The King is expecting you. Come right in."

Peg-a-leg marched proudly in through the door, along the thick, rich carpet of a long hall, and into the royal reception room, with the black velvet bag held before him in both hands. The carpet led him between people on the left side of the reception room and people on the right, all the way up to the throne where the King sat waiting in his stocking feet. Beside him sat the Queen waiting patiently. Peg-a-leg strutted up to the King, bowed, and knelt on one knee before him.

"Your Majesty," said Peg-a-leg, "I, Peg-a-leg, the finest cobbler in all Dunsoon, am about to present to *you* the most unusual pair of shoes in all the world."

With this, Peg-a-leg reached into his bag and took out a shoe. He gave it to the King, who looked at it inside and out and passed it to the Queen. The Queen said, "It looks all right, but I hope it wears well. We can't be getting you a pair of new shoes each and every week, you know."

It was a very lovely shoe. The people at the front of the room near the throne got a glimpse of it and murmured, "Oh!" and "Ah!" The people in the middle of the room could not tell what the shoe looked like except that it was a shoe, but they, too, murmured their "ah's" and "oh's." From the back of the room no one could see a thing, yet, each one exclaimed his "ah" and "oh" and added as well, "How pretty!"

The shoe came back at last to Peg-a-leg who said, "By your leave, Your Majesty." He took the King's left foot, rested it on his knee, and put the shoe on it. The King snuggled his foot in it a bit and waited while Peg-a-leg laced it up and tied a neat bow. Then the King stood up, tried the shoe this way and that, walked up and down the carpet, and sat down again.

"The shoe fits very well, Peg-a-leg," declared the King. "Not bad—not bad at all. I hope the other shoe fits as well."

A smile of pleasure shone on Peg-a-leg's face. He proudly took the other shoe out of the bag, rested the

King's right foot on his knee, and tried to put on the shoe. Here was something strange—the shoe would not go on! Peg-a-leg gave it a little jerk. That did not do it. He gave it a great jerk. Still the shoe did not go on. Peg-a-leg gave the shoe such a strong jerk that he almost jerked the King off his throne. Even that did not do it.

"What is this?" Peg-a-leg asked himself. "Can it be that I have made the shoe too tight? That's odd! I never did anything like that before. Can it be that the stocking is wrinkled?"

A worried look came on Peg-a-leg's face. This would never, never do. He took off the shoe and looked at it inside and out. Nothing seemed to be wrong with it. He looked at the King's stocking. That, too, was as it should be. He loosened the lace to the very bottom and tried again.

It was no use. The shoe would not go on!

Everyone was waiting. The King looked down at Peg-a-leg and waited. The Queen tapped her foot impatiently, and said, "Hm!"

Someone asked, "What's the matter?"

To this, someone else said, "Perhaps the shoe does not fit."

"Impossible!" he was told. "Who ever heard of Peg-a-leg making a shoe that did not fit?"

Still the shoe did not go on.

Peg-a-leg took the shoe off the King's foot and put it beside the one on the King's left foot. Peg-a-leg looked at both shoes and his face got red—as red as the carpet on the floor.

"You—you—Your Ma–ma–ma–majesty!" Peg-a-leg stammered.

"Yes, Peg-a-leg?"

"I don't know how it happened, Your Majesty. It never happened before in all my days. I can't see how it happened this time."

"Well, well, tell us and be done. What is it that has happened?"

"Your Majesty," faltered Peg-a-leg, "I am awfully sorry. I am ashamed to say it but–but–I must have made a mistake and made both shoes for the left foot."

The Queen tittered. The King roared with

laughter. Everyone roared with laughter as the news passed from the people near the throne to the people in the middle of the room, to the people in the farthest corners. "Think of it!" they said, "Peg-a-leg has made two left shoes! Two left shoes! Think of it, two left shoes!"

The laughter swelled and swelled until it seemed to rise in a great wave that picked up Peg-a-leg and his two left shoes, carried him down the red carpet, out of the palace, along the road, and left him at the very door of his little shop.

Peg-a-leg locked himself in his shop and went to work. In a short time he had another shoe finished. "This will do it," he said. He put the shoe beside the other shoes and almost died of the shock.

Do you know what he had done? He could not explain it. He could not tell how it had happened, but he had made another left shoe.

"Oh, this is awful! This is terrible!" he exclaimed. "Now I'll have to make three right shoes to match the three left shoes."

It was night. It was late. All of Dunsoon slept. There was not a light showing anywhere. That is, nowhere except the faint crack of light under the shutters of the windows of the shop where Peg-a-leg worked like mad to make three right shoes.

When the cold, grey light of dawn wove itself into the dusk of the tree-tops, Peg-a-leg had the three shoes finished. His eyes were so weary that he could hardly see. His hands were so tired they could hardly hold the shoes. He set each of the three shoes beside one of the left shoes. "Now I can go to sleep," said Peg-a-leg. But, even as he said it, he blinked his eyes and almost fainted at the sight. Each left shoe instead of having a right shoe for a partner had another left shoe!

There was nothing left to do but to go to bed.

There was no more leather left. There was no more thread left. There was not a lace left. The only things left were the six left shoes.

Peg-a-leg went to sleep and dreamed that long rows of shoes, each one a left shoe, paraded by him and laughed at him and stuck their tongues out at him. He did not sleep very long. He could not sleep very long. He got up, washed, grabbed a bit of breakfast, and hurried to the market to buy more leather, pegs, laces, thread, needles, and a new sharp knife. He came back to the shop and laid out the patterns for six right shoes. He worked and worked until the six shoes were finished and set alongside of the six left shoes.

Was everything right this time?

No! Each of the latest six shoes also was a left shoe.

Poor Peg-a-leg! What was he to do?

He set to work and made twelve shoes. They, too, were left shoes and, now, he had twenty-four shoes all of the same size and made to fit the King's left foot.

Peg-a-leg tried and tried again. Do what he would, he simply could not make a right shoe. Every shoe he made turned out to be a left shoe. There were left shoes on all his shelves. There were left shoes on his counter. There were left shoes on the floor, in the window, and there even was a left shoe sticking out of Peg-a-leg's left back pocket. Forty, fifty, sixty, seventy, seventy-one shoes were crowded into Peg-a-leg's shop before Peg-a-leg realized that, somehow, he could not make a right shoe.

Perhaps it was the excitement. It might be that a spell was upon him because he had been too greedy. Perhaps he was too anxious and was trying too hard. Whatever it was, it seemed that Peg-a-leg had lost the trick of making right shoes. He could make only left ones.

There was nothing to do but tell the King about his trouble. He got a big sack, put the seventy-one left shoes into it, and set out to tell the King. He tried to get into the castle by the back door but the sack was so big that he had to be allowed to come in the front door.

The King said to him, "Well, Peg-a-leg, are my shoes finished at last?"

Peg-a-leg answered not a word. Instead, he began taking shoes out of his sack and placed them around the King in a great circle, all seventy-one of them. The King looked at each one in turn as it was taken out and set down and his wonder grew and grew.

"What joke is this, Peg-a-leg?" the King demanded sternly. "What in the world is the use of seventy-one left shoes without a right shoe to match one of them?"

"Your Majesty," said Peg-a-leg sorrowfully, "if this is a joke, it is a joke that has frightened me almost to death! It seems that I cannot make a right shoe. As you see, every shoe I have made turns out to be a left shoe. What am I to do?"

"Do?" cried the King. "I suppose the only thing to do is to have you bring your tools and leather right here and let you make me a right shoe while I watch you. This time, I wager, you won't make a left shoe."

Peg-a-leg ran home to his little shop as fast as he could. He came running back with his tools, leather, lasts, and all the things that he might need to make a right shoe for the King.

"That shoe won't dare be anything but right with the King watching it!" said Peg-a-leg as he ran.

The King and the Queen sat on their thrones. The courtiers, lords, and ladies looked on with great interest. They had never seen a shoe being made before. Peg-a-leg spread his things around him on the floor near the throne and worked as he had never worked before. His knife flashed. His needle flew in and out. His hammer pegged rap-rap-rap. A half hour, an hour, two hours, two hours and fourteen minutes went by. At last the shoe was finished. Peg-a-leg fell back on the floor, too spent even to take the shoe to the King. Instead, a lord picked it up, took the shoe to the King, and tried to help him on with it.

The King lifted his right foot, put it into the shoe as far as he could, and, suddenly, kicked it straight up into the air so that it sailed across the entire room and flew out through an open window.

Peg-a-leg, even with the King and all the court watching him, had made still another left shoe.

"Peg-a-leg!" roared the King. "This time you have gone too far. This is no longer a joke. For this you shall be hanged! There is no place in Dunsoon for a workman who makes a jest of his work."

Peg-a-leg wept with shame and sorrow. "You are right, Your Majesty. I deserve to die. I'm truly sorry. After I am gone I hope you will forget this sad failure of mine and think only of the times I made shoes for you that pleased you."

At this speech no one could keep the tears from coming into his eyes.

Poor Peg-a-leg! He sat on the floor looking so sad, lonely, and miserable that the King felt sorry for him and got off his throne and sat down on the lowest step of the short flight of stairs leading up to the throne.

"What is more," said the King to Peg-a-leg, "I am disappointed. The King of Runnyrun is coming to pay me a visit in a few days and I wanted to wear my new shoes for him. I'll bet *he* has a pair of new shoes when he comes to visit me. Now I'll have to wear these old ones. Peg-a-leg, I didn't think you would do this to your friend, the King. I am very sorry for you, but I shall have to hang you just the same. There is nothing else that I can do. You know how it is with kings."

Peg-a-leg was taken away and locked up in the dungeon under the palace. With him were locked up his tools and the seventy-two left shoes. He sat in his cell and was sorry for his fate. He wondered and wondered how this strange thing could have happened.

"If only I had not been so greedy!" he told himself. "If I had not been so greedy, I would not have been so excited. If I had not been so excited, I would not have forgotten how to make a right shoe."

But there it was. He was so downhearted that he did not even think of trying to make another right shoe again. What was the use? He was going to die! All day long he heard the sound of a strange hammering in the courtyard. Peg-a-leg guessed that they were building the gallows on which he was to be hanged the next morning.

He was right. Late in the afternoon, when the sun was low in the sky, the long shadow of the gallows stretched itself across the courtyard outside his window. The shadow of the noose was there too. It frightened Peg-a-leg as it crept steadily toward him. He imagined that he could feel it already tightening about his throat.

"No! No!" he pleaded. "Take it away! Don't let it come near me! I do not want to die! Must a man die just because he has forgotten how to make a right shoe? I'll remember again! Give me another chance!"

The next day was cool, but it was bright with sunshine. All the people of Dunsoon, it seemed, both great and small, were crowded into the courtyard. There was little or no talking. Everyone was wide-eyed, sober, and solemn. Even the birds sensed what was about to happen and had stilled their song. The King and Queen were there. The King was nervous. He did not like the business at all. The Queen looked as if she had been crying.

Over to one side, poor Dilly stood and cried and cried as if her heart would break. Over and over she kept saying, "Oh, I knew something awful would happen because Peg-a-leg was greedy. I knew something awful would happen! How I wish I could help my poor Peg-a-leg!"

Peg-a-leg was led out of his cell. He walked slowly through the courtyard and mounted the steps leading up to the gallows. The seventy-two shoes, together with his cobbler-tools, were put around him as silent witnesses of his guilt. Just before the noose was put about his neck, the King came over to him and said, "I am sorry, Peg-a-leg. Believe me, I am sorry.

This will leave us without a single cobbler in all Dunsoon. However, you know that you have failed your King, your country, and your trade. For this you must die. But, since it is the custom to grant a dying man one last wish, you may ask for anything in my power to grant you. Peg-a-leg, name your last wish."

Peg-a-leg raised his head to the soft sunshine. It was too good a world to be leaving it. He wished that it were raining instead. Or, at least, that it might have been cloudy. He searched through the crowd until he found Dilly. As he watched her, he saw her do a strange—a very strange thing. Peg-a-leg saw his wife nervously peel off the glove from her left hand so that it was turned completely inside out. Then she just as nervously peeled off the glove from her right hand so that it, too, was turned completely inside out. Still watching her, Peg-a-leg saw her begin to put the gloves on again. But the strange thing was that now the left glove had become a right glove and the right glove had

become a left glove. Strangest of all, the gloves fitted as well worn inside out as they had when they were worn outside out.

A second time Dilly peeled off her gloves and put them on again. A third time she did it. Peg-a-leg watched her wide-eyed. All at once he got the meaning of what she was doing. Quick as an indrawn breath the thought came to him. It hit him, swept through him, and pulled his mind up with a jerk.

"Wait a minute!" he told himself. "Can it be? Is it? It must be!" he decided. "If Dilly can make her left glove into a right glove that she can wear on her right hand by turning it inside out, why can't I take a left shoe, turn it inside out, and make it into a right shoe? Of course I can. I can! I can! I can do it!" he shouted.

He turned to the King and said, "Your Majesty, this is my last wish. Give me but one more chance to make a right shoe. This time I know I can do it!"

The King hesitated for a moment. "Very well, Peg-a-leg," he said, "your last wish is granted."

The noose was taken off Peg-a-leg's neck. He jumped up, grabbed one of the left shoes, took a knife, ripped off the sole, turned the upper part of the shoe inside out, turned the sole over, and sewed all together again.

"I've done it!" exclaimed Peg-a-leg shaking with excitement. Tears of joy ran down his face. "I've done it! At last I can make a right shoe."

There was no mistake about it this time. The spell was broken. To prove it, Peg-a-leg ran and picked up another shoe. He turned it into a right shoe, too. He did this to thirty-six of the left shoes and thus had thirty-six pairs of shoes, right ones as well as left ones. There they sat, all thirty-six pairs of them, as innocent as could be, in a great circle on the platform of the gallows. Thirty-six pairs of shoes! All of one size! All made to fit the King.

The King tried on one right shoe. He tried on another right shoe. He tried on every right shoe. Each right shoe fitted perfectly. "You are pardoned, Peg-a-leg," he declared, beaming with happiness.

What a shout of joy and gladness went up from everyone! "Hurrah for Peg-a-leg!" they shouted. "Hurrah for the King! Hurrah for Peg-a-leg!"

There was but one thing to do with the thirty-six pairs of shoes. It was up to Peg-a-leg and he did it. He turned to the King and said, "Your Majesty, this is a great day for me. I shall make it a great day for you, too. To mark the saving of my life, I shall make you a thank-you-gift of every one of the thirty-six pairs of new shoes."

The King could hardly believe his ears. "Thirty-six pairs of brand-new shoes!" he exclaimed. "Now I really am a king. Thank you, Peg-a-leg. You are most unselfish. And since you are so generous, I can be no

less generous than you are. I make you a present of this ring and do hereby appoint you for ever and ever, Lord Cobbler to the King of Dunsoon."

Saying this, the King took a great diamond ring from his little finger and gave it to Peg-a-leg.

"Thank you, Your Majesty! Thank you! Thank you! Thank you!" said Peg-a-leg overcome with joy. "I shall be happy to be Lord Cobbler. But this ring—no, I cannot keep this ring for myself. I should give it to my wife, Dilly, for saving my life."

Peg-a-leg excused himself. Without wasting a single moment, he quickly ran over to where Dilly was waiting, all full of smiles and happiness, and gave her the diamond ring.

If it was a great day for Peg-a-leg, it was an especially great day for the King. For the first time in history, the King of Dunsoon had not two, not ten, not twenty, but thirty-six pairs of brand-new shoes at one and the same time. What made it even more wonderful was that they had all been made by Peg-a-leg, Lord Cobbler to the King; Peg-a-leg who was still the best, the greatest, the cleverest, and above all, the most generous cobbler in all Dunsoon.

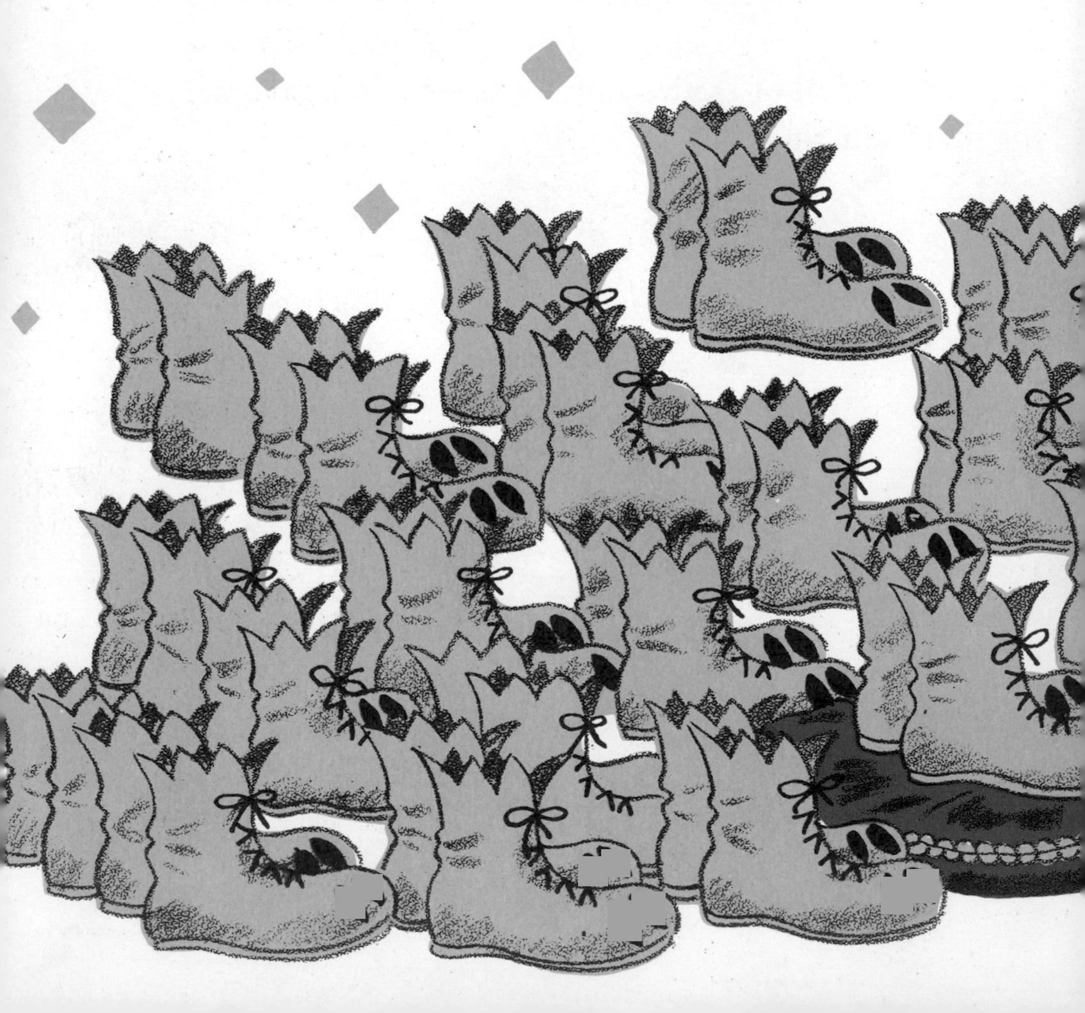

A FAVORE REGIS NOMEN
Peg-a-leg
4656